THE WIND BLEW

THE WIND BLEW

PAT HUTCHINS

Macmillan Publishing Company

New York

Macmillan Publishing Co., Inc., 866 Third Avenue, New York, N.Y. 10022
Collier Macmillan Canada, Inc.
Library of Congress catalog card number: 73–11691
Printed in the United States of America

10   9   8

The illustrations are full-color tempera paintings.
The typeface is Korinna, with the display set in Quaint Open.

Library of Congress Cataloging in Publication Data

Hutchins, Pat, date   The wind blew.   [1.   Stories in rhyme]   I.   Title.
PZ8.3.H965Wi   811'.5'4 [E]   73–11691   ISBN 0–02–745910–1

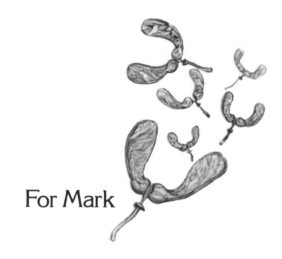

For Mark

The wind blew.

It took the umbrella from Mr. White
and quickly turned it inside out.

It snatched the balloon from little Priscilla
and swept it up to join the umbrella.

And not content, it took a hat,
and still not satisfied with that,

it whipped a kite into the air
and kept it spinning round up there.

It grabbed a shirt left out to dry
and tossed it upward to the sky.

It plucked a hanky from a nose
and up and up and up it rose.

It lifted the wig from the judge's head
and didn't drop it back. Instead

it whirled the postman's letters up,
as if it hadn't done enough.

It blew so hard it quickly stole
a striped flag fluttering on a pole.

It pulled the new scarves from the twins and tossed them to the other things.

It sent the newspapers fluttering round,
then tired of the things it found,

it mixed them up

and threw them down

and blew away to sea.